The Spicy Soun

Jim Harmon

Alpha Editions

This edition published in 2024

ISBN : 9789361476051

Design and Setting By
Alpha Editions
www.alphaedis.com
Email - info@alphaedis.com

THE SPICY SOUND OF SUCCESS

By JIM HARMON

*Now was the captain's chance to prove he knew
less than the crew—all their lives hung upon it!*

There was nothing showing on the video screen. That was why we were looking at it so analytically.

"Transphasia, that's what it is," Ordinary Spaceman Quade stated with a definite thrust of his angular jaw in my direction. "You can take my word on that, Captain Gavin."

"Can't," I told him. "I can't trust your opinion. I can't trust *anything*. That's why I'm Captain."

"You'll get over feeling like that."

"I know. Then I'll become First Officer."

"But look at that screen, sir," Quade said with an emphatic swing of his scarred arm. "I've seen blank scanning like that before and you haven't—it's your first trip. This always means transphasia—cortex dissolution, motor area feedback, the Aitchell Effect—call it anything you like, it's still transphasia."

"I know what transphasia is," I said moderately. "It means an electrogravitational disturbance of incoming sense data, rechanneling it to the wrong receptive areas. Besides the human brain, it also effects electronic equipment, like radar and television."

"Obviously." Quade glanced disgustedly at the screen.

"Too obvious. This time it might not be a familiar condition of many planetary gravitational fields. On this planet, that blank kinescope may mean our Big Brother kites were knocked down by hostile natives."

"You are plain wrong, Captain. Traditionally, alien races never interfere with our explorations. Generally, they are so alien to us they can't even recognize our existence."

I drew myself up to my full height—and noticed in irritation it was still an inch less than Quade's. "I don't understand you men. Look at yourself, Quade. You've been busted to Ordinary Spaceman for just that kind of thinking, for relying on tradition, on things that have worked before. Not only your thinking is slipshod, you've grown careless about everything else, even your own life."

"Just a minute, Captain. I've never been 'busted.' In the Exploration Service, we regard Ordinary Spaceman as our highest rank. With my hazard pay, I get more hard cash than *you* do, and I'm closer to retirement."

"That's a shallow excuse for complacency."

"Complacency! I've seen ten thousand wonders in twenty years of space, with a million variations. But the patterns repeat themselves. We learn to know what to expect, so maybe we can't maintain the reactionary caution the service likes in officers."

"I resent the word 'reactionary,' Spaceman! In civilian life, I was a lapidary and I learned the value of deliberation. But I never got too cataleptic to tap a million-dollar gem, which is more than my contemporaries can say, many of 'em."

"Captain Gavin," Quade said patiently, "you must realize that an outsider like you, among a crew of skilled spacemen, can never be more than a figurehead."

Was this the way I was to be treated? Why, this man had deliberately insulted me, his captain. I controlled myself, remembering the familiarity that had always existed between members of a crew working under close conditions, from the time of the ancient submarines and the first orbital ships.

"Quade," I said, "there's only one way for us to find out which of us is right about the cause of our scanning blackout."

"We go out and find the reason."

"Exactly. We go. You and me. I hope you can stand my company."

"I'm not sure I can," he answered reluctantly. "My hazard pay doesn't cover exploring with rookies. With all due respect, Captain."

I clapped him on the shoulder. "But, man, you have just been telling me all we had to worry about was common transphasia. A man with your experience could protect himself and cover even a rookie, under such familiar conditions—right?"

"Yes, sir, I suppose I could," Quade said, bitterly aware he had lost out somewhere and hoping that it wasn't the start of a trend.

"Looks okay to me," I said. Quade passed a gauntlet over his faceplate. "It's real. I can blur it with a smudged visor. When it blurs, it's solid."

The landscape beyond the black corona left by our landing rockets was unimpressive. The rocky desert was made up of silicon and iron oxide, so it looked much the same as a terrestrial location. Yellowish-white sand ran up to and around reddish brown rock clawing into the pink sunlight.

"I don't understand it," Quade admitted. "Transphasia hits you a foul as soon as you let it into the airlock."

"Apparently, Quade, *this* thing is going to creep up on us."

"Don't sound smug, Captain. It's pitty-pattying behind you too."

The keening call across the surface of consciousness postponed my reply.

The wail was ominously forlorn, defiant of description. I turned my head around slowly inside my helmet, not even sure that I had heard it.

But what else can you do with a wail but *hear* it?

Quade nodded. "I've felt this before. It usually hits sooner. Let's trace it."

"I don't like this," I admitted. "It's not at all what I expected from what you said about transphasia. It must be something else."

"It couldn't be anything else. I know what to expect. You don't. You may begin smelling sensations, tasting sounds, hearing sights, seeing tastes, touching odors—or any other combination. Don't let it bother you."

"Of course not. I'll soothe my nerves by counting little shocks of lanolin jumping over a loud fence."

Quade grinned behind his faceplate. "Good idea."

"Then you can have it. I'm going to try keeping my eyes open and staying alive."

There was no reply.

His expression was tart and greasy despite all his light talk, and I knew mine was the same. I tested the security rope between our pressure suits. It was a taut and virile bass.

We scaled a staccato of rocks, our suits grinding pepper against our hides.

The musk summit rose before us, a minor-key horizon with a shifting treble for as far as I could smell. It was primitive beauty that made you feel shocking pink inside. The most beautiful vista I had ever tasted, it couldn't be dulled even by the sensation of beef broth under my skin.

"Is this transphasia?" I asked in awe.

"It always has been before," Quade remarked. "Ready to swallow your words about this being something an old hand wouldn't recognize, Captain?"

"I'm swallowing no words until I find out precisely how they taste here."

"Not a bad taste. They're pretty. Or haven't you noticed?"

"Quade, you're right! About the colors anyway. This reminds me of an illiscope recording from a cybernetic translator."

"It should. I don't suppose we could understand each other if it wasn't for our morphistudy courses in reading cross-sense translations of Centauri blushtalk and the like."

It became difficult to understand him, difficult to try talking in the face of such splendor. You never really appreciate colors until you smell them for the first time.

Quade was as conversational as ever, though. "I can't see irregularities occurring in a gravitational field. We must have compensated for the transphasia while we still had a point of reference, the solid reality of the spaceship. But out here, where all we have to hang onto is each other, our concept of reality goes *bang* and deflates to a tired joke."

Before I could agree with one of his theories for once, a streak of spice shot past us. It bounced back tangily and made a bitter rip between the two of us. There was no time to judge its size, if it had size, or its decibel range, or its caloric count, before a small, sharp pain dug in and dwindled down to nothing in one long second.

The new odor pattern in my head told me Quade was saying something I couldn't quite make out.

Quade then pulled me in the direction of the nasty little pain.

"Wait a minute, Spaceman!" I bellowed. "Where the devil do you think you're dragging me? Halt! That's a direct order."

He stopped. "Don't you want to find out what that was? This *is* an exploration party, you know, sir."

"I'm not sure I do want to find out what that was just now. I didn't like the feel of it. But the important thing is for us not to get any further from the ship."

"That's important, Captain?"

"To the best of my judgment, yes. This—condition—didn't begin until we got so far away from the spacer—in time or distance. I don't want it to get any worse. It's troublesome not to know black from white, but it would be a downright inconvenience not to know which way is up."

"Not for an experienced spaceman," Quade griped. "I'm used to free-fall."

But he turned back.

"Just a minute," I said. "There was something strange up ahead. I want to see if short-range radar can get through our electrogravitational jamming here."

I took a sighting. My helmet set projected the pattern on the cornea. Sweetness building up to a stab of pure salt—those were the blips.

Beside me, there was a thin thread of violet. Quade had whistled. He was reading the map too.

The slope fell away sharply in front of us, becoming a deep gorge. There was something broken and twisted at the bottom, something we had known for an instant as a streak of spice.

"There's one free-fall," I said, "where you wouldn't live long enough to get used to it."

He said nothing on the route back to the spacer.

"I know all about this sort of thing, Gav," First Officer Nagurski said expansively. He was rubbing the well-worn ears of our beagle mascot, Bruce. A heavy tail thudded on the steel deck from time to time.

My finger could barely get in the chafing band of my regulation collar. I was hot and tired, fresh—in only the chronological sense—from a pressure suit.

"What do you know all about, Nagurski? Dogs? Spacemen? Women? Transphasia?"

"Yes," he answered casually. "But I had immediate reference to our current psychophysiological phenomenon."

I collapsed into the swivel in front of the chart table. "First off, let's hear what you know about—never mind, make it dogs."

"Take Bruce, for example, then—"

"No, thanks. I was wondering why *you* did."

"I didn't." His dark, round face was bland. "Bruce picked me. Followed me home one night in Chicago Port. The dog or the man who picks his own master is the most content."

"Bruce is content," I admitted. "He couldn't be any more content and still be alive. But I'm not sure that theory works out with men. We'd have anarchy if I tried to let these starbucks pick their own master."

"*I* had no trouble when I was a captain," Nagurski said. "Ease the reins on the men. Just offer them your advice, your guidance. They will soon see why the service selected you as captain; they will pick you themselves."

"Did your crew voluntarily elect you as their leader?"

"Of course they did, Gav. I'm an old hand at controlling crews."

"Then why are you First Officer under me now?"

He blinked, then decided to laugh. "I've been in space a good many years. I really wanted to relax a little bit more. Besides, the increase in hazard pay was actually more than my salary as a captain. I'm a notch nearer retirement too."

"Tell me, did you always feel this way about letting the men select their own leader?"

Nagurski brought out a pipe. He would have a pipe, I decided.

"No, not always. I was like you at first. Fresh from the cosmic energy test lab, suspicious of everything, trying to tell the old hands what to do. But I learned that they are pretty smart boys; they know what they are doing. You can rely on them absolutely."

I leaned forward, elbows on knees. "Let me tell *you* a thing, Nagurski. Your trust of these damn-fool spacemen is why you are no longer a captain. You can't trust anything out here in space, much less human nature. Even I know that much!"

He was pained. "If you don't trust the men, they won't trust you, Gav."

"They don't have to trust me. All they have to do is *obey* me or, by Jupiter, get frozen stiff and thawed out just in time for court-marshal back home. Listen," I continued earnestly, "these men aren't going to think of me—of *us*, the officers, as their leaders. As far as the crew is concerned, Ordinary Spaceman Quade is the best man on this ship."

"He *is* a good man," Nagurski said. "You mustn't be jealous of his status."

The dog growled. He must have sensed what I almost did to Nagurski.

"Never mind that for now," I said wearily. "What was your idea for getting our exploration parties through this transphasia?"

"There's only one idea for that," said Quade, ducking his long head and stepping through the connecting hatch. "With the Captain's permission...."

"Go ahead, Quade, tell him," Nagurski invited.

"There's only one way to wade through transphasia with any reliability," Quade told me. "You keep some kind of physical contact with the spaceship. Parties are strung out on guide line, like we were, but the cable has to be run back and made fast to the hull."

"How far can we run it back?"

Quade shrugged. "Miles."

"How many?"

"We have three miles of cable. As long as you can feel, taste, see, smell or hear that rope anchoring you to home, you aren't lost."

"Three miles isn't good enough. We don't have enough fuel to change sites that often. You can't use the drive in a gravitational field, you know."

"What else can we do, Captain?" Nagurski asked puzzledly.

"You've said that the spaceship is our only protection from transphasia. Is that it?"

Quade gave a curt nod.

"Then," I told them, "we will have to start tearing apart this ship."

Sergeant-Major Hoffman and his team were doing a good job of ripping out the side of the afterhold. Through the portal I could see the suited men expertly guiding the huge curved sections on their ray projectors.

"Cannibalizing is dangerous." Nagurski put his pipe in his teeth and shook his head disapprovingly.

"Spaceships have parts as interchangeable as Erector sets. We can take apart the tractors and put our ship back together again after we complete the survey."

"You can't assemble a jigsaw puzzle if some of the pieces are missing."

"You can't get a complete picture, but you can get a good idea of what it looks like. We can take off in a reasonable facsimile of a spaceship."

"Not," he persisted, "if *too* many parts are missing."

"Nagurski, if you are looking for a job safer than space exploration, why don't you go back to testing cosmic bomb shelters?"

Nagurski flushed. "Look here, Captain, you are being too damned cautious. There is a way one handles the survey of a planet like this, and this isn't the way."

"It's my way. You heard what Quade said. You know it yourself. The men have to have something tangible to hang onto out there. One slender cable isn't enough of an edge on sensory anarchy. If the product of their own technological civilization can keep them sane, I say let 'em take a part of that environment with them."

"In departing from standard procedure that we have learned to trust, you are risking more than a few men—you risk the whole mission in gambling so much of the ship. A captain doesn't take chances like that!"

"I never said I wouldn't take chances. But I'm not going to take *stupid* chances. I *might* be doing the wrong thing, but I can see you *would* be doing it wrong."

"You know nothing about space, Captain! You have to trust *us*."

"That's it exactly, First Officer Nagurski," I said sociably. "If you lazy, lax, complacent slobs want to do something in a particular way, I know it *has* to be wrong."

I turned and found Wallace, the personnel man, standing in the hatchway.

"Pardon, Captain, but would you say we also lacked initiative?"

"I would," I answered levelly.

"Then you'll be interested to hear that Spaceman Quade took a suit and a cartographer unit. He's out there somewhere, alone."

"The idiot!" I yelped. "Everyone needs a partner out there. Send out a team to follow his cable and drag him in here by it."

"He didn't hook on a cable, Captain," Wallace said. "I suppose he intended to go beyond the three-mile limit as you demanded."

"Shut up, Wallace. You don't have to like me, but you can't twist what I said as long as I command this spacer."

"Cool off, Gav," Nagurski advised me. "It's been done before. Anybody else would have been a fool to go out alone, but Quade is the most experienced man we have. He knows transphasia. Trust him."

"I trusted him too far by letting him run around loose. He needs a leash in more ways than one, and I'm going to put one on him."

For me, it was a nightmare. I lay down in my cabin and thought. I had to think things through very carefully. One mistake was too many for me. My worst fear had been that someday I would overlook one tiny flaw and ruin a gem. Now I might have ruined an exploration and destroyed a man, not a stone, because I had missed the flaw.

No one but a reckless fool would have gone out alone on a strange planet with a terrifying phenomenon, but I'd had enough evidence to see that space exploration *made* a man a reckless fool by doing things on one planet he had once found safe and wise on some other world.

The thought intruded itself: *why* hadn't I recognized this before I let Quade escape to almost certain death? Wasn't it because I wanted him dead, because I resented the crew's resentment of my authority, and recognized in him the leader and symbol of this resentment?

I threw away that idea along with my half-used cigarette. It might very well be true, but how did that help now?

I had to *think*.

I was going after him, that was certain. Not only for humane reasons—he was the most important member of the crew. With him around, there were only two opinions, his and mine. Without him, I'd have endless opinions to contend with.

But it wouldn't do any good to go out no better equipped than he. There was no time to wait for tractors to be built if we wanted to reach him alive, and we certainly couldn't reach him five or ten miles out with our three miles of safety line. We would have to go in spacesuits.

But how would that leave us any better off than Quade?

Why was Quade vulnerable in his spacesuit, as I knew from experience he would be?

How could we be less vulnerable, or preferably invulnerable?

"Captain, you got nothing to worry about," Quartermaster Farley said. He patted a space helmet paternally. "You got yourself a self-contained environment. The suit's eye looks into yours at the arteries in the back of your eyeball so it can read your amber corpuscles and feed you your oxygen in the right amounts; you're a bottle-fed baby. If transphasia gets you seeing limburger, turn on the radar and you're air-conditioned as an igloo. Nothing short of a cosmic blast can dent that hide. You got it made."

"You are right," I said, "only transphasia comes right through these air-fast joints."

"Something strange about the trance, Captain," Farley said darkly. "Any spaceman can tell you that. Things we don't understand."

"I'm talking about something we do understand—*sound*. These suits perfectly soundproof?"

"Well, you can pick up sound by conduction. Like putting two helmets together and talking without using radio. You can't insulate enough to block out all sound and still have a man-shaped suit. You have—"

"I know. Then you have something like a tractor or a miniature spaceship. There isn't time for that. We will have to live with the sound."

"What do you think he's going to hear out there, Captain? We'd like to find one of those beautiful sirens on some planet, believe me, but—"

"I believe you," I said quickly. "Let's leave it at that. I don't know what he will hear; what's worrying me is *how* he'll hear it, in what sensory medium. I hope the sound doesn't blind him. His radar is his only chance."

"How do you figure on getting a better edge yourself, sir?"

"I have the idea, but not the word for it. Tonal compensation, I suppose. If you can't shut out the noise, we'll have to drown it out."

Farley nodded. "Beat like a telephone time signal?"

"That would do it."

"It would do something else. It would drive you nuts."

I shrugged. "It might be distracting."

"Captain, take my word for it," argued Farley. "Constant sonic feedback inside a spacesuit will set you rocking against the grain."

"Devise some regular system of interruptions," I suggested.

"Then the pattern will drive you crazy. Maybe in a few months, with luck, I could plan some harmonic scale you could tolerate—"

"We don't have a few months," I said. "How about music? There's a harmonic scale for you, and we can endure it, some of it. *Figaro* and *Asleep in the Cradle of the Deep* can compensate for high-pitched outside temperatures, and *Flight of the Bumble Bee* to block bass notes."

Farley nodded. "Might work. I can program the tapes from the library."

"Good. There's one more thing—how are our stores of medicinal liquor?"

Farley paled. "Captain, are you implying that *I* should be running short on alcohol? Where do you get off suggesting a thing like that?"

"I'm getting off at the right stop, apparently," I sighed. "Okay, Farley, no evasions. In plain figures, how much drinking alcohol do we have left?"

The quartermaster slumped a bit. "Twenty-one liters unbroken. One more about half full."

"Half full? How did that ever happen? I mean you had some *left*? We'll take this up later. I want you to run it through the synthesizer to get some light wine...."

"Light wine?" Farley looked in pain. "Not whiskey, brandy, beer?"

"Light wine. Then ration it out to some of the men."

"Ration it to the men!"

"That's an accurate interpretation of my orders."

"But, sir," Farley protested, "you don't give alcohol to the crew in the middle of a mission. It's not done. What reason can you have?"

"To sharpen their taste and olfactory senses. We can turn up or block out sound. We can use radar to extend our sight, but the Space Service hasn't yet developed anything to make spacemen taste or smell better."

"They are going to smell like a herd of winos," Farley said. "I don't like to think how they would taste."

"It's an entirely practical idea. Tea-tasters used to drink almond-and-barley water to sharpen their senses. I've observed that wine helps you appreciate culinary art more. Considering the mixed-up sensory data under transphasia, wine may help us to see where we are going."

"Yes, sir," Farley said obediently. "I'll give spacemen a few quarts of wine, telling them to use it carefully for scientific purposes only, and then they will be able to see where they are going. Yes, sir."

I turned to leave, then paused briefly. "You can come along, Farley. I'm sure you want to see that we don't waste any of the stuff."

"There they are!" Nagurski called. "Quade's footsteps again, just beyond that rocky ridge."

The landscape was rich chocolate ice cream smothered with chocolate syrup, caramel, peanuts and maple syrup, eaten while you smoked an old, mellow Havana. The footsteps were faint traces of whipped cream across the dark, rich taste of the planet.

I splashed some wine from my drinking tube against the roof of my mouth to sharpen my taste. It brought out the footsteps sharper. It also made the landscape more of a teen-ager's caloric nightmare.

The four of us pulled ourselves closer together by reeling in more of our safety line. Farley and Hoffman, Nagurski and myself, we were cabled together. It gave us a larger hunk of reality to hold onto. Even so, things wavered for me during a wisp of time.

We stumbled over the ridge, feeling out the territory. It was a sticky job crawling over a melting, chunk-style Hershey bar. I was thankful for the invigorating Sousa march blasting inside my helmet. Before the tape had cut in, kicked on by the decibel gauge, I had heard or felt something dark and ominous in the outside air.

"Yes, this is definitely the trail of Quail," Nagurski said soberly. "This is serious business. I must ask whoever has been giggling on this channel to shut up. Pardon me, Captain. *You* weren't giggling, sir?"

"I have never giggled in my life, Nagurski."

"Yes, sir. That's what we all thought."

A moment later, Nagurski added, "Anyway, I just noticed it was my shelf—my, that is, self."

The basso profundo performing *Figaro* on my headset climbed to a girlish shriek. A sliver of ice. This was the call Quade and I had first heard as we were about to troop over a cliff. I dug in my heels.

"Take a good look around, boys," I said. "What do you see?"

"Quail," Nagurski replied. "That's what I see."

"You," I said carefully, "have been in space a *long* time. Look again."

"I see our old buddy, Quail."

I took another slosh of burgundy and peered up ahead. It *was* Quade. A man in a spacesuit, faceplate in the dust, two hundred yards ahead.

Grudgingly I stepped forward, out of the shadow of the ridge. A hysterically screaming wind rocked me on my toes. We pushed on sluggishly to Quade's side, moving to the tempo of *Pomp and Circumstance*.

Farley lugged Quade over on his back and read his gauges.

The Quartermaster rose with grim deliberation, and hiccuped. "Better get him back to the spaceship fast. I've seen this kind of thing before with transphasia. His body cooled down because of the screaming wind—psychosomatic reaction—and his heating circuits compensated for the cool flesh. The poor devil's got frostbite and heat prostration."

The four of us managed to haul Quade back by using the powered joints in our suits. Hoffman suggested that he had once seen an injured man walked back inside his suit like a robot, but it was a delicate adjustment, controlling power circuits from outside a suit. It was too much for us—we were too tired, too numb, too drunk.

At first sight of the spacer in the distance, transphasia left me with only a chocolate-tasting pink after-image on my retina. It was now showing bare skeleton from cannibalization for tractor parts, but it looked good to me, like home.

The wailing call sounded through the amber twilight.

I realized that I was actually *hearing* it for the first time.

The alien stood between us and the ship. It was a great pot-bellied lizard as tall as a man. Its sound came from a flat, vibrating beaver tail. Others of its kind were coming into view behind it.

"Stand your ground," I warned the others thickly. "They may be dangerous."

Quade sat up on our crisscross litter of arms. "Aliens can't be hostile. Ethnic impossibility. I'll show you."

Quade was delirious and we were drunk. He got away from us and jogged toward the herd.

"Let's give him a hand!" Farley shouted. "We'll take us a specimen!"

I couldn't stop them. Being in Alpine rope with them, I went along. At the time, it even seemed vaguely like a good idea.

As we lumbered toward them, the aliens fell back in a solid line except for the first curious-looking one. Quade got there ahead of us and made a grab. The creature rose into the air with a screaming vibration of his tail and landed on top of him, flattening him instantly.

"Sssh, men," Nagurski said. "Leave it to me. I'll surround him."

The men followed the First Officer's example, and the rope tying them to him. I went along cheerfully myself, until an enormous rump struck me violently in the face. My leaded boots were driven down into fertile soil, and my helmet was ringing like a bell. I got a jerky picture of the beast jumping up and down on top of the others joyously. Only the stiff space armor was holding up our slack frames.

"Let's let him escape," Hoffman suggested on the audio circuit.

"I'd like to," Nagurski admitted, "but the other beasts won't let us get past their circle."

It was true. The aliens formed a ring around us, and each time a bouncing boy hit the line, he only bounced back on top of us.

"Flat!" I yelled. "Our seams can't take much more of this beating."

I followed my own advice and landed in the dirt beside Quade.

The bouncer came to rest and regarded us silently, head on an eighty-degree angle.

I was stone sober.

The others were lying around me quietly, passed out, knocked out, or taking cover.

The ring of aliens drew in about us, closer, tighter, as the bouncer sat on his haunches and waited for us to move.

"Feeling better?" I asked Quade in the infirmary.

He punched up his pillow and settled back. "I guess so. But when I think of all the ways I nearly got myself killed out there.... How far have you got in the tractors?"

"I'm having the tractors torn down and the parts put back into the spaceship where they belong. We *shouldn't* risk losing them and getting stuck here."

"Are you settling for a primary exploration?"

"No. I think I had the right idea on your rescue party. You have to meet and fight a planet on its own terms. Fighting confused sounds and tastes with music and wine was crude, but it was on the right track. Out there, we understood language because we were familiar with alien languages changed to other sense mediums by cybernetic translators. Using the translator, we can learn to recognize all confused data as easily. I'm starting indoctrination courses."

"I doubt that that is necessary, sir," Quade said. "Experienced spacemen are experienced with transphasia. You don't have to worry. In the future, I'll be able to resist sensations that tell me I'm freezing to death—if my gauges tell me it's a lie."

I examined his bandisprayed hide. "I think my way of gaining experience is less painful and more efficient."

Quade squirmed. "Yes, sir. One thing, sir—I don't understand how you got me away from those aliens."

"The aliens were trying to help. They knew something was wrong and they were prodding and probing. When the first tractor pulled up and the men got out, they seemed to realize our own people could help us easier than they could."

"I am not quite convinced that those babies just meant to help us all the time."

"But they did! First, that call of theirs—it wasn't to lead us into danger, but to warn us of the cliff, the freezing wind. They saw we were trying to find out things about their world, so they even offered us one of their own kind to study. Unfortunately, he was too much for us. They didn't give us their top man, of course, only the village idiot. It's just as well. We aren't allowed to dissect creatures that far up the intelligence scale."

"But why should they want to help us?" Quade demanded suspiciously.

"I think it's like Nagurski's dog. The dog came to him when it wanted somebody to own it, protect it, feed it, love it. These aliens *want* Earthmen to colonize the planet. We came here, you see, same as the dog came to Nagurski."

"Well, I've learned one thing from all of this," Quade said. "I've been a blind, arrogant, cocksure fool, following courses that were good on *some* worlds, *most* worlds, but not good on *all* worlds. I'm never going to be that foolhardy again."

"But you're losing *confidence*, Quade! You aren't sure of yourself any more. Isn't confidence a spaceman's most valuable asset?"

"The hell it is," Quade said grimly. "It's his deadliest liability."

"In that case, I must inform you that I am demoting you to Acting Executive Officer."

"Huh?" Quade gawked. "But dammit, Captain, you can't do that to me! I'll lose hazard pay and be that much further from retirement!"

"That's tough," I sympathized, "but in every service a chap gets broken in rank now and then."

"Maybe it's worth it," Quade said heavily. "Now maybe I've learned how to stay alive out here. I just hope I don't forget."

I thought about that. I was nearly through with my first mission and I could speak with experience, even if it was the least amount of experience aboard.

"Quade," I said, "space isn't as dangerous as all that." I clapped him on the shoulder fraternally. "You worry too much!"